This Winnie-the-Pooh book belongs to

....

EGMONT
We bring stories to life

This edition first published in Great Britain in 2018
Originally published in Great Britain 2017 by Egmont UK Limited
The Yellow Building, 1 Nicholas Road, London W11 4AN

Written by Jane Riordan
Designed by Pritty Ramjee
Illustrated by Eleanor Taylor and Mikki Butterley
Copyright © 2018 Disney Enterprises, Inc.
Based on the "Winnie the Pooh" works
by A.A.Milne and E.H.Shepard

ISBN 978 1 4052 9110 1
68737/001
Printed in Italy

Winnie-the-Pooh
A Tree for Christmas

EGMONT

"I saw in a book," said Winnie-the-Pooh, one wintery day as he sat in his cosy little house with Piglet, "that at Christmas you should have a **tree** in your house, covered with decorations and lights and looking **Wonderful.**"

"A tree in a house?" replied Piglet, a little confused. "But I live in a tree."

"Ah, yes," said Pooh, "and so do I — this will be trickier than I thought. We'd better ask Owl."

"A tree in a tree!" exclaimed Owl, when they'd explained everything to him. "That's not right at all. I've heard of ships in bottles but never trees in trees. Trees live in forests and we live in trees and that's all there is to say about it."

"I suppose if it were a very small one, it might fit," ventured Piglet.

"In a bottle?" asked Pooh, who hadn't quite been paying attention.

"Through the door," said Piglet. "Come on, let's go and **hunt** for one."

So they said
goodbye to Owl
and headed out
into the cold
to hunt for the
type of tree
that might fit
through a door.

"Too **tall.**"

"Too **wide**."

"Too **spiky**. Ouch!"

"What we need," said Pooh, "is a Not Very Grown Tree and not very much grows at Eeyore's Gloomy Place so let's try there."

But all they found was a gloomy-looking Eeyore and some gloomy-looking thistles.

The thistles would certainly fit through a door but didn't somehow have that

Christmassy
            Wonderfulness

that they were hoping for.

They had just about given up and
were on their way home for a little
smackerel of something, when they
came to a clearing and in the middle
they saw ... **the tree**...

Not too **tall**.

Not too **wide**.

Not too **spiky**.

And just the right size to fit through a door.

"And now we must get it home," said Pooh.

He pulled.

And Piglet pushed.

But the little tree didn't want to be moved. It seemed quite happy where it was.

By now, nearly everyone in the Hundred Acre Wood had heard about the great Christmas Tree Hunt and they had all gathered to help.

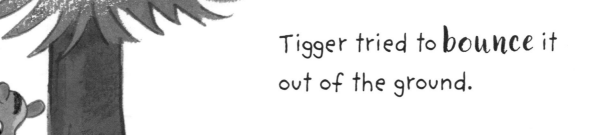

Tigger tried to **bounce** it out of the ground.

Rabbit tried to **nibble** through the trunk.

And Kanga spoke very firmly to the tree, saying,
"That's quite enough fuss."

But the tree stayed exactly where it was.

Just at that moment, the first flakes of snow began to fall and Christopher Robin came whistling through the Forest.

"Hallo, everyone," he said, brightly, and then he saw their dejected faces. "Why, what's the matter? Cheer up, it's nearly Christmas."

"Exactly," sighed Pooh. "It's nearly Christmas and we haven't got a tree looking all **Christmassy** and **Wonderful.** We found this one but it wants to stay here in the Forest."

"Oh, I see," said Christopher Robin. "Well, if the tree won't come for Christmas, then we'll bring Christmas to the tree."

And so it was decided and Rabbit waved his arms a great deal and gave everyone a job.

Pooh gathered **pine cones**.

Piglet found **haycorns**.

Owl
went
home
to
fetch
various
candle ends.

Tigger bounced high into the trees to gather **mistletoe.**

Kanga and Roo picked bright **red berries.**

Eeyore offered his back as a lowish stool and Christopher Robin hung everything on their little tree.

Then, very carefully, Christopher Robin lit the candles.

Roo squeaked and squealed with delight.

"**Stand back, Roo dear,**" worried Kanga.

The sun had just set in the Hundred Acre Wood and the tree looked simply **Wonderful**. The candles flickered in the breeze and bounced light all around the clearing.

"This little tree," announced Christopher Robin solemnly, "is Our Christmas Tree. Pooh Bear and Piglet found it and everyone else helped. We must meet here every Christmas and every year I will have grown," he glanced at little Piglet, "and others not so much. But the tree will certainly keep growing because it knew that the Forest was the best place of all for it to be."

And they all cheered and wished each other a Very Merry Christmas.

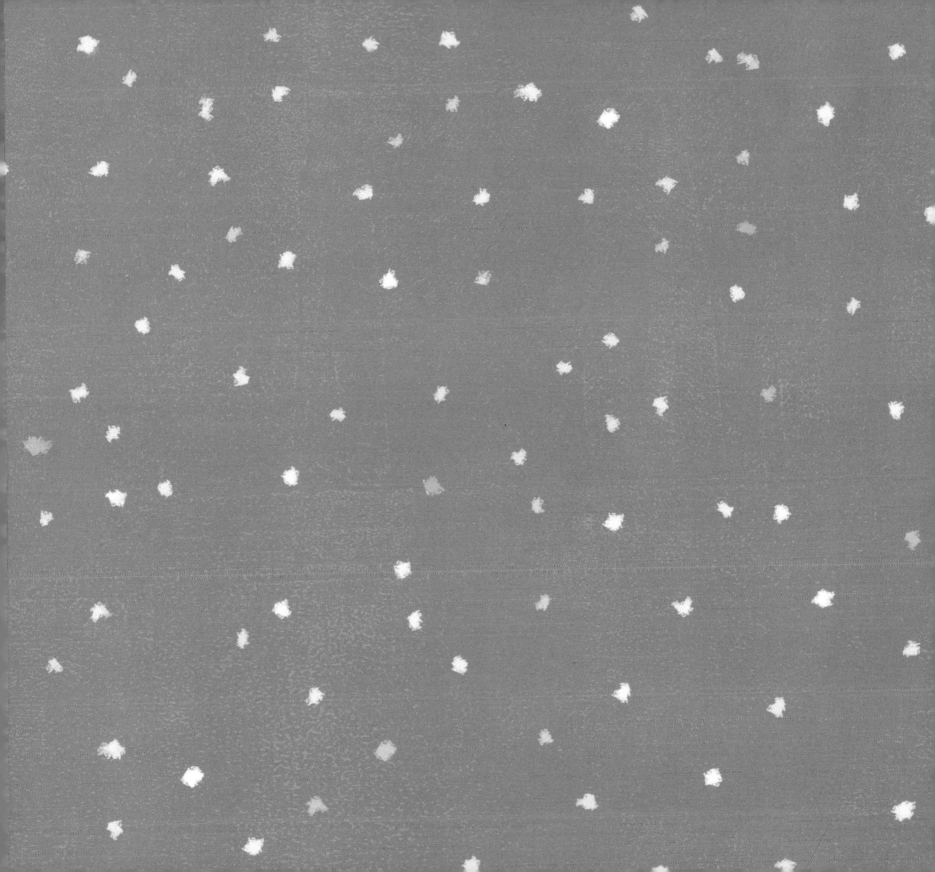

Winnie-the-Pooh
The Great Heffalump Hunt

A delightful tale of Heffalumps, bravery and large jars of honey.
Inspired by the classic tales of A.A.Milne

Winnie-the-Pooh

The
Great
Heffalump
Hunt

Giles Andreae

From the author of
Giraffes Can't Dance

EGMONT